This
Treasure Cove Story
belongs to

**CAPTAIN AMERICA
HIGH-STAKES HEIST!**

A CENTUM BOOK 978-1-912396-75-7
Published in Great Britain by Centum Books Ltd.
This edition published 2018.

1 3 5 7 9 10 8 6 4 2

Centum Books Ltd, 20 Devon Square, Newton Abbot,
Devon, TQ12 2HR, UK.

www.centumbooksltd.co.uk | books@centumbooksltd.co.uk
CENTUM BOOKS Limited Reg.No. 07641486.

A CIP catalogue record for this book is available
from the British Library.

Printed in China.

centum

A Treasure Cove Story

MARVEL
CAPTAIN AMERICA

HIGH-STAKES HEIST!

Based on the stories by Marvel Comics
By Courtney Carbone
Illustrated by Michael Borkowski and Michael Atiyeh

Early one morning, the superhero Captain America and his sidekick, Bucky Barnes, were on patrol at the US Mint in Washington, DC.

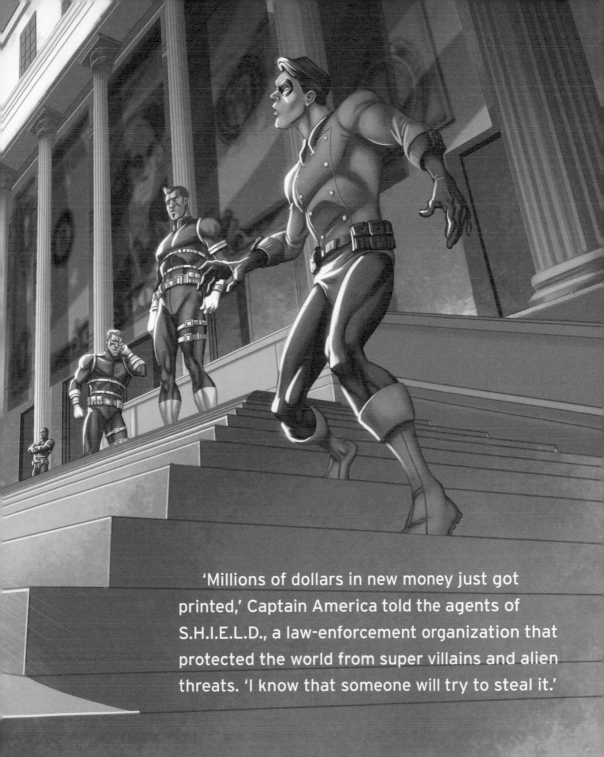

'Millions of dollars in new money just got printed,' Captain America told the agents of S.H.I.E.L.D., a law-enforcement organization that protected the world from super villains and alien threats. 'I know that someone will try to steal it.'

Suddenly, energy blasts erupted from the sky! Moving swiftly, Captain America used his indestructible shield to protect Bucky.

'Quick! Get behind me,' Captain America shouted.

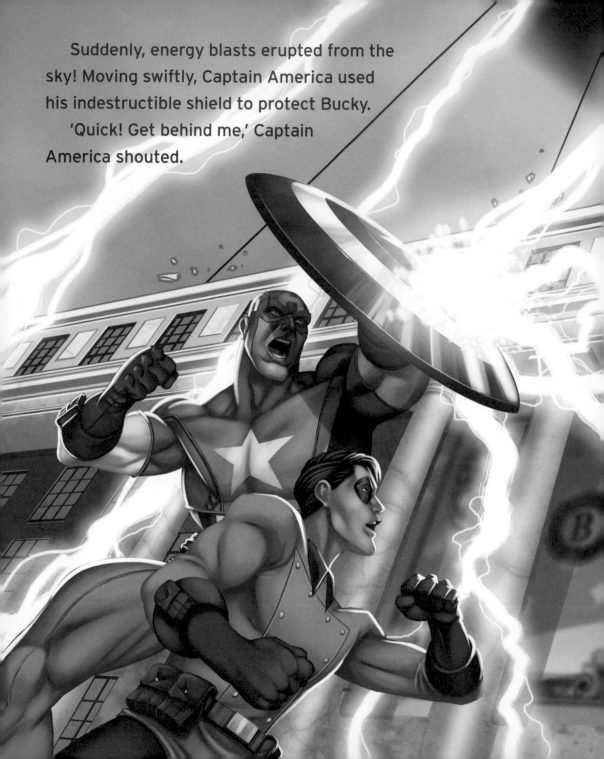

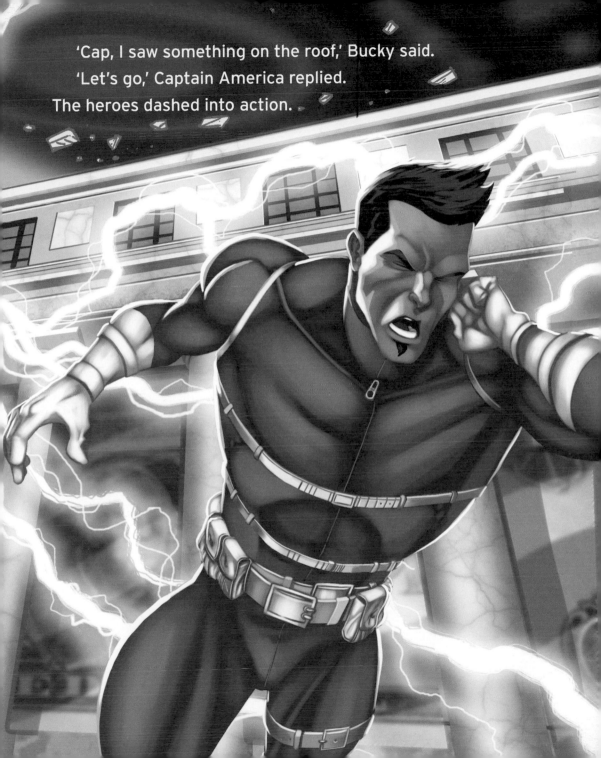

'Cap, I saw something on the roof,' Bucky said.
'Let's go,' Captain America replied.
The heroes dashed into action.

'The doors are locked from the inside,' said Bucky.
'Follow me!' Captain America shouted as he began
to climb the building.

'They tore off the roof!' Bucky exclaimed.

'Somebody really wants those new bills,' Captain America said. 'Let's find out who it is – and stop them!'

'Get every last dollar,' a robotic villain barked at his monster-men. 'I will use these riches in my plans to take over the world!'

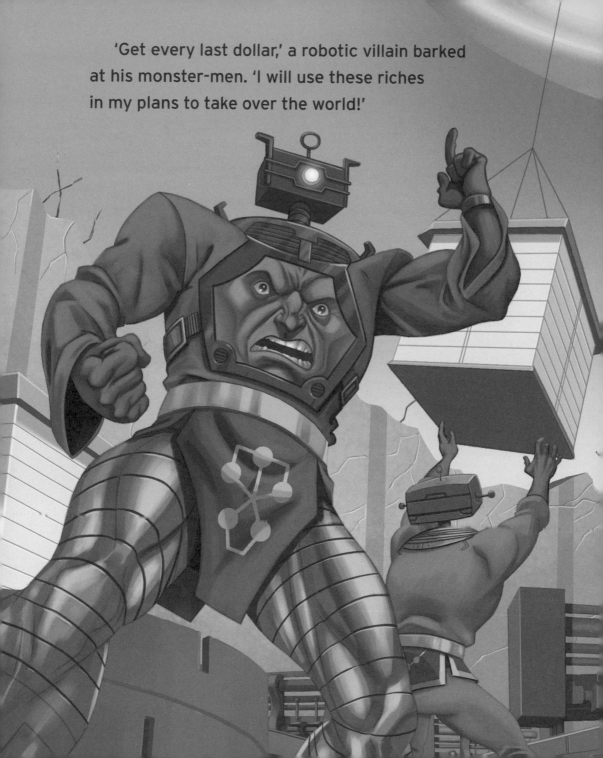

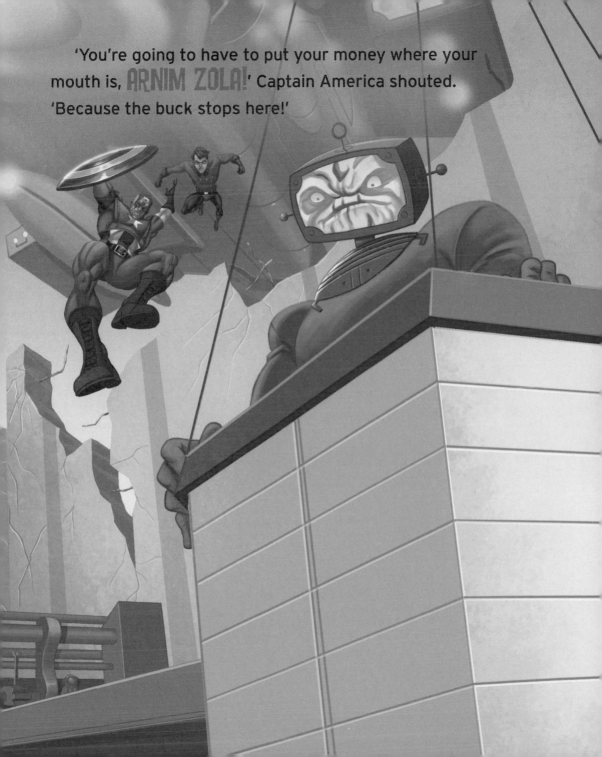

'You're a day late and a dollar short, Captain
- my monster-men are more than a match for you,'
Arnim Zola replied. 'Get them!'

The monster-men lumbered forward.

'I hope this fight doesn't cost us an arm and a leg,' Bucky joked.

The monster-men were no match for Captain America and Bucky. Arnim Zola's creatures were strong, but the heroes were too fast and too skilled at fighting.

'Time to pay the piper, Zola!' Captain America said, stopping the last monster-man with his shield.

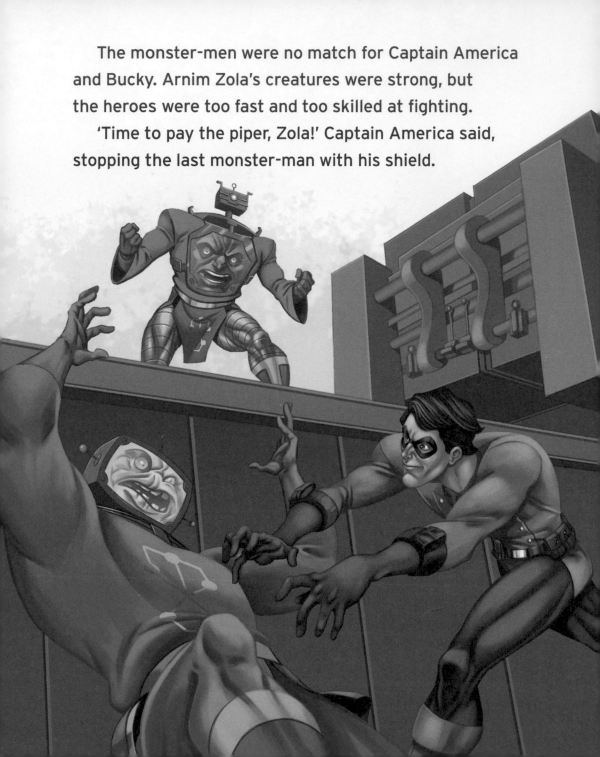

Without warning, Arnim Zola projected a powerful mind-control beam at Bucky. 'There's one person you can't defeat,' the villain said, laughing. 'I will make your best friend your worst foe!'

The young hero's eyes turned white and he began moving like a zombie towards Captain America!

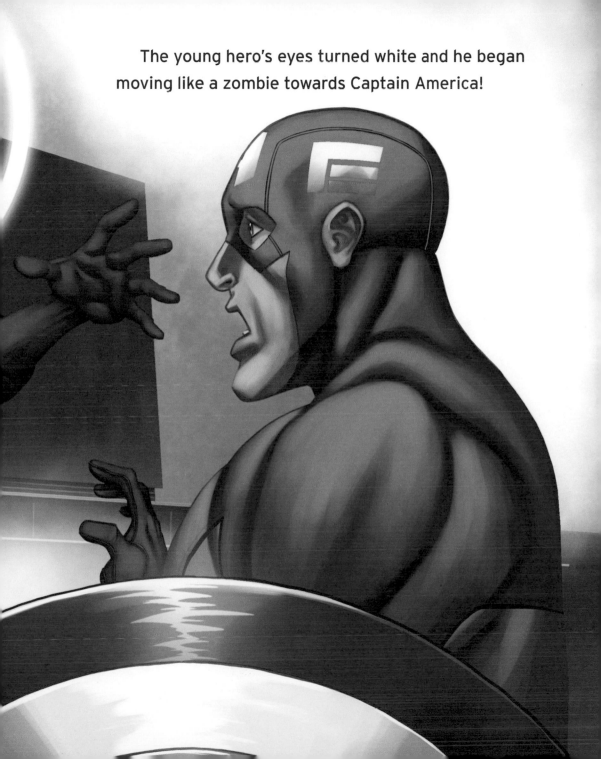

Bucky grabbed Captain America in a vice-like grip. 'Bucky, it's me, Cap!' the hero pleaded. He didn't want to hurt his friend. 'We have to stop Zola!'

'With the mind-controlling powers of my ESP box,' Zola bragged, 'no one can stop me. Not even you, Captain America!'

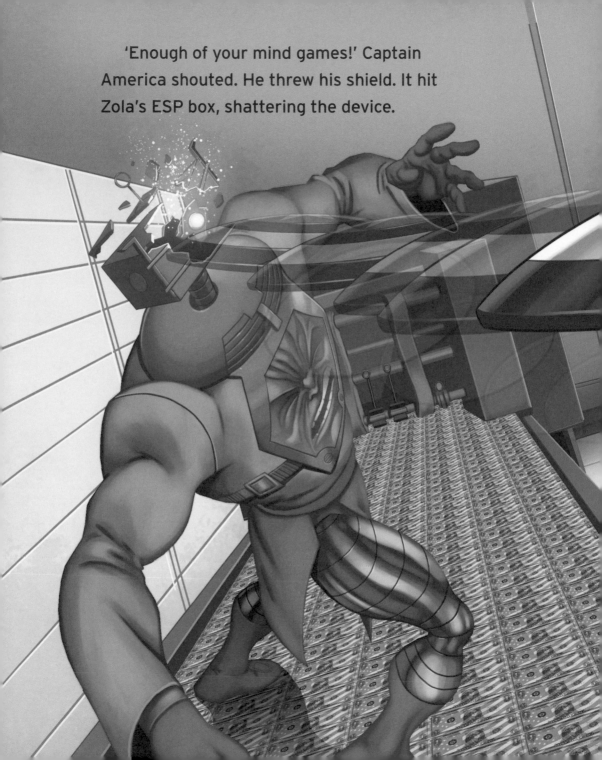

'Enough of your mind games!' Captain America shouted. He threw his shield. It hit Zola's ESP box, shattering the device.

Captain America's shield bounced off the villain and hit the printing press' controls. The machine roared to life!

Arnim Zola's feet flew out from under him...

THUMP! ...and he was sucked into the printing press!

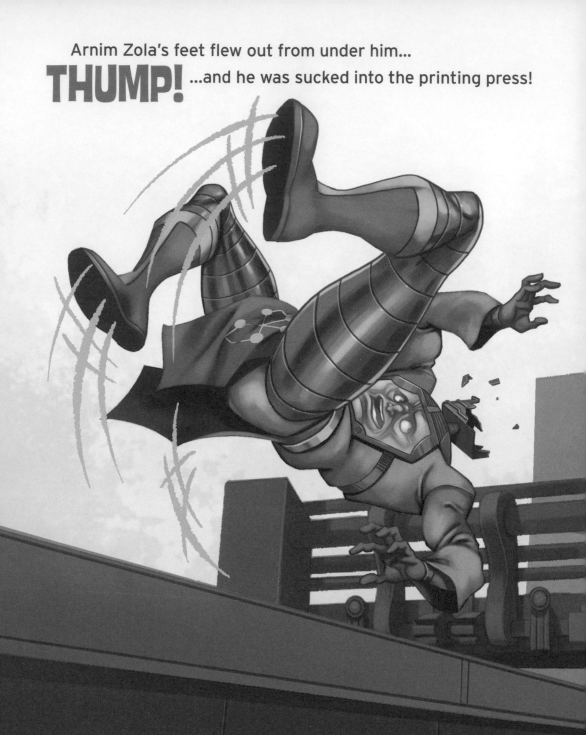

Pssssst!

Zola was covered in green ink...

CLANG!

slapped with metal printing plates...

THUNK!

and bound with sturdy bands!

Bucky unlocked the front door for the S.H.I.E.L.D. agents.
Captain America handed the super villain over to them.

'Looks like Arnim Zola learned that crime doesn't pay,'
Captain America said as Bucky held up a dollar bill printed
with Zola's face. 'Now he's going to **spend** his time in jail.'

Treasure Cove Stories

1 Three Little Pigs
2 Snow White and
The Seven Dwarfs
3 The Fox and the Hound
- Hide-and-Seek
4 Dumbo
5 Cinderella
6 Cinderella's Friends
7 Alice in Wonderland
8 Mad Hatter's Tea Party
from Alice in Wonderland
9 Mickey Mouse and
his Spaceship
10 Peter Pan
11 Pinocchio
12 The Prince and the Pauper
13 Sleeping Beauty
and the Good Fairies
14 The Lucky Puppy
15 Chicken Little
16 Santa's Toy Shop
17 Coco
18 Winnie-the-Pooh
and Tigger
19 The Sword in the Stone
20 Mary Poppins
21 The Jungle Book
22 The Aristocats
23 Lady and the Tramp
24 Bambi
25 Bambi - Friends of the Forest
26 Pete's Dragon
27 Beauty and the Beast
- The Teapot's Tale
28 Monsters, Inc.
- M is for Monster
29 Finding Nemo
30 The Incredibles
31 The Incredibles
- Jack-Jack Attack
32 Ratatouille
- Your Friend the Rat
33 Wall·E
34 Up
35 Princess and the Frog
36 Toy Story - The Pet Problem
37 Dora the Explorer
- Dora and the Unicorn King

38 Dora the Explorer
- Grandma's House
39 Spider-Man
- Night of the Vulture!
40 Wreck-it Ralph
41 Brave
42 The Invincible Iron Man
- Eye of the Dragon
43 SpongeBob SquarePants
- Sponge in Space!
44 SpongeBob SquarePants
- Where the Pirates Arrrgh!
45 Toy Story
- A Roaring Adventure
46 Cars - Deputy Mater
Saves the Day!
47 Spider-Man
- Trapped By The Green Goblin!
48 Big Hero 6
49 Spider-Man - High Voltage!
50 Frozen
51 Cinderella Is My Babysitter
52 Beauty and the Beast
- I Am The Beast
53 Blaze and the Monster
Machines - Mighty Monster
Machines
54 Blaze and the Monster
Machines - Dino Parade!
55 Teenage Mutant Ninja Turtles
- Follow The Ninja!
56 I Am A Princess
57 Paw Patrol
- The Big Book of Paw Patrol
58 Paw Patrol
- Adventures with Grandpa!
59 Merida Is Our Babysitter
60 Trolls
61 Trolls Holiday Special
62 The Secret Life of Pets
63 Zootropolis
64 Ariel Is My Babysitter
65 Inside Out
66 Belle Is My Babysitter
67 The Lion Guard
- Eye In The Sky
68 Moana
69 Finding Dory

70 Guardians of the Galaxy
71 Captain America
- High-Stakes Heist!
72 Ant-Man
73 The Mighty Avengers
74 The Mighty Avengers
- Lights Out!
75 The Incredible Hulk
76 Shimmer & Shine
- Wish upon a Sleepover
77 Shimmer & Shine
- Backyard Ballet
78 Paw Patrol - All-Star Pups!
79 Teenage Mutant Ninja Turtles
- Really Spaced Out!
80 Cars 2 - Travel Buddies
81 Madagascar
82 Jasmine Is My Babysitter
83 How To Train Your Dragon
84 Shrek
85 Puss In Boots
86 Kung Fu Panda
87 Beauty and the Beast
- I Am Belle
88 The Lion Guard
- The Imaginary Okapi
89 Thor - Thunder Strike!
90 Guardians of the Galaxy
-Rocket to the Rescue!
91 Nella The Princess Knight
- Nella and the Dragon
92 Shimmer & Shine
- Treasure Twins!
93 Olaf's Frozen Adventure
94 Black Panther
95 Branch's Bunker Birthday
96 Shimmer & Shine
- Pet Talent Show
97 The Ugly Duckling
98 Look Out for Mater!
99 101 Dalmatians
100 The Sorcerer's Apprentice
101 Tangled
102 Vampirina
- The Littlest Vampire
103 Puppy Dog Pals
- Don't Rain on my Pug-Rade

•Book list may be subject to change.